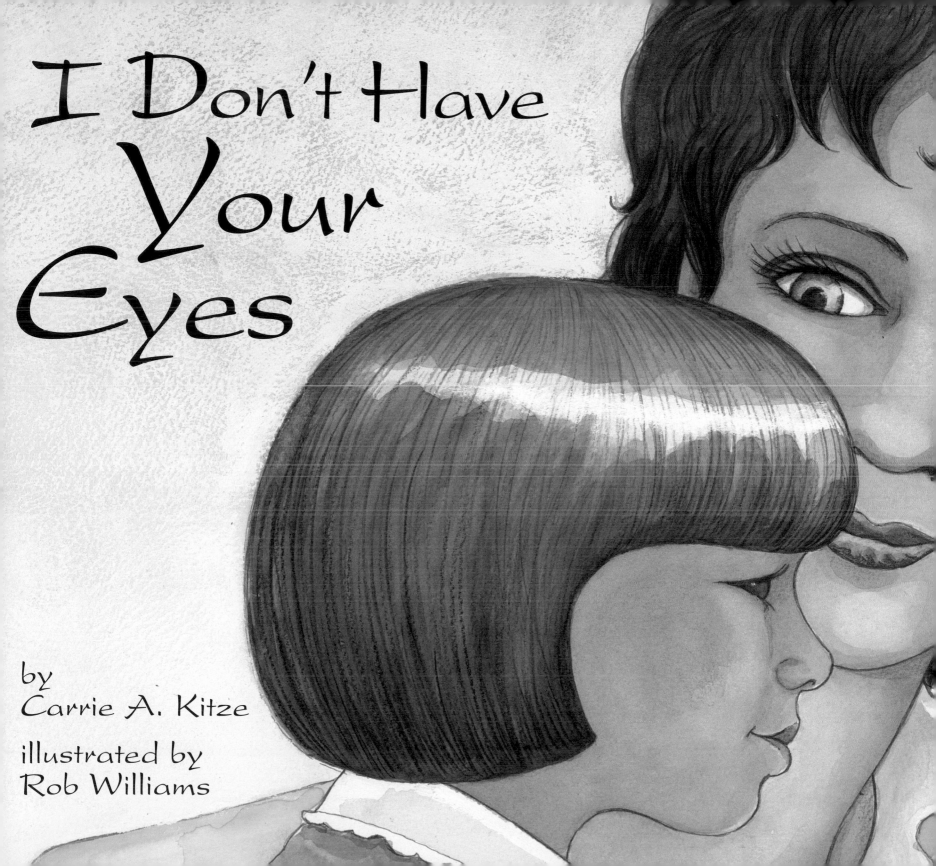

I Don't Have Your Eyes

by
Carrie A. Kitze

illustrated by
Rob Williams

Published by:
EMK Press,
a division of EMK Group, LLC
16 Mt Bethel Road, #219
Warren, NJ 07059
www.emkpress.com

Known as the "Toolbox Press", we create resources for families touched by adoption and foster care. We also raise funds for children who remain in orphanages or foster care situations worldwide, and for adoption information programs domestically.

Publisher's Cataloging-in-Publication
(provided by Quality Books, Inc.)
Kitze, Carrie A.
   I don't have your eyes / by Carrie A. Kitze :
 illustrated by Rob Williams. -- 1st ed.
   p. cm.
   SUMMARY: Gental multicultural exploration of how
 people are alike despite differences in appearance,
 background or ethnicity.
   Audience: Ages 2-5
   LCCN 2001012345
   ISBN 0972624422
   ISBN-13 978-0-9726244-2-8
1. Individual differences--Juvenile fiction.
2. Identity (Psychology)--Juvenile fiction.
3. Ethnicity--Juvenile Fiction. [1. Individuality– Fiction.
2. Ethnicity--Fiction] I. Williams, Rob.
II. Title.

PZ7.K6728Ido 2003   [E]
              QB133-1572

First Edition, November 2003. Second printing, May 2007, Third printing September 2011

Printed in USA
printed on acid free paper, library binding

EMK Press titles currently in print:

The Foster Parenting Toolbox
Edited by Kim Phagan Hansel

Adoption Parenting: Creating a Toolbox,
Building Connections
Edited by Sheena Macrae and Jean MacLeod

Forever Fingerprints
by Sherrie Eldridge

Pieces of Me: Who Do I Want to Be?
Voices for and by adopted teens
edited by Robert L. Ballard, PhD

We See the Moon
by Carrie Kitze

At Home in This World,
A China Adoption Story
by Jean MacLeod

We publish books for adoptive and
foster families.
We provide a wealth of resources and web links on our site that are available for free download, and a monthly newsletter on topics of interest to adoptive and foster families.
For a guide on how to use this book and some activities to do with groups of
children to talk about differences, visit the school resources area on our website.

www.emkpress.com

To reach us via email:

info@emkpress.com

Connections are vitally important to children as they begin to find their place in the world. For transracial and transcultural adoptees, and for children in foster care or kinship placements, celebrating the differences within their families as well as the similarities that connect them, is the foundation for belonging. As parents or caregivers, we can strengthen our children's tie to family and embrace the differences that make them unique. Each child has their own story and their own special place to belong.

For my family,
Rob, Annette, and Natalie.
In our hearts we are the same.

C.A.K.

For the most important people to me
on the planet...
Eileen, Sarah, Chris, and Emily

R.W.

I don't have your eyes . . .

. . . but
I have
your way of
looking at things.

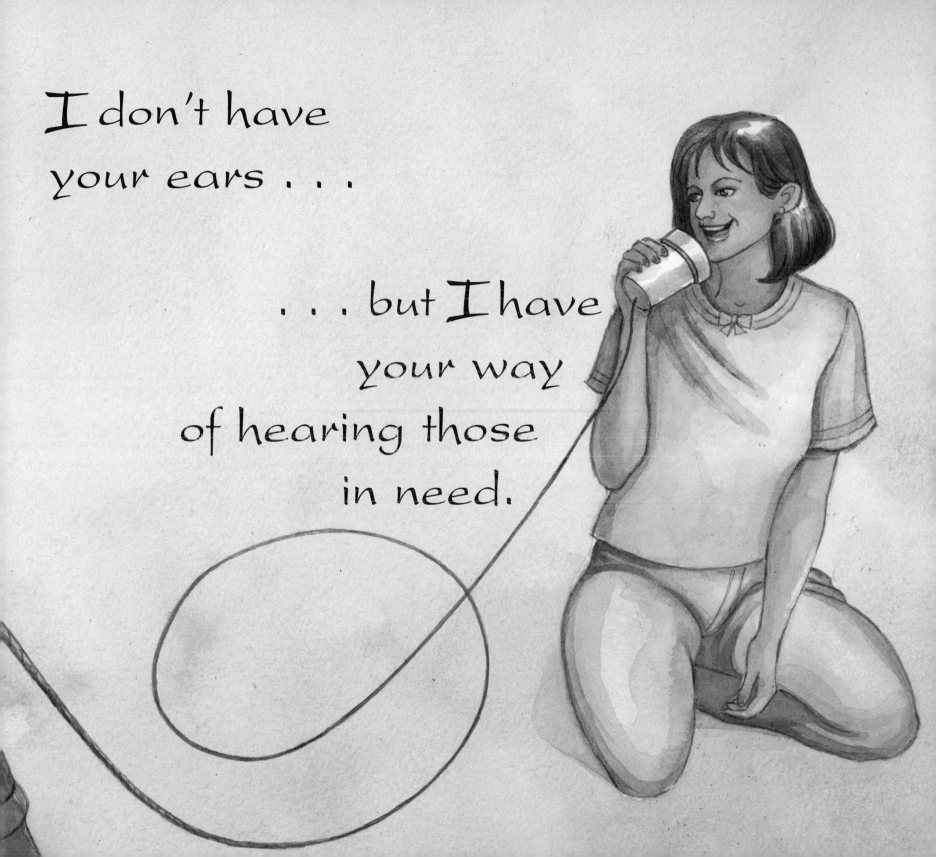

I don't have your nose . . .

. . .but I have your way of stopping and smelling the flowers.

I don't have your hair . . .

. . . but
I have

your way
of letting it down!

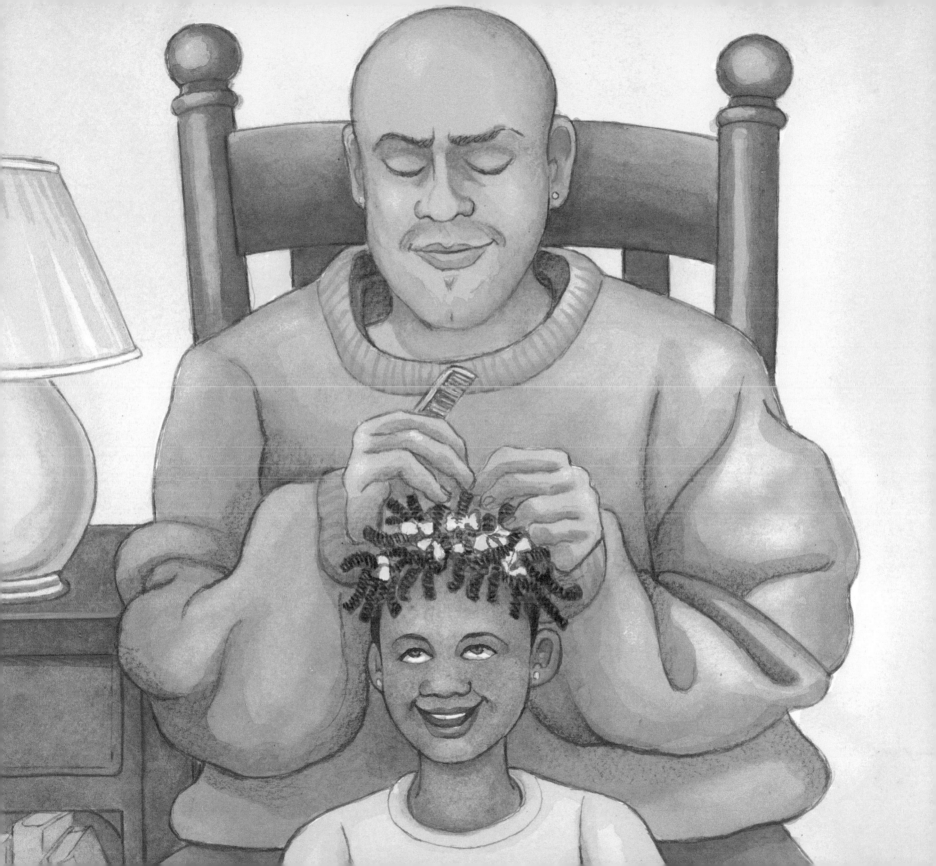

I don't have your hands . . .

. . . but I have

your way of gently
touching others.

I don't have your knees . . .

. . . but I have
learned your way
of giving thanks
on mine.

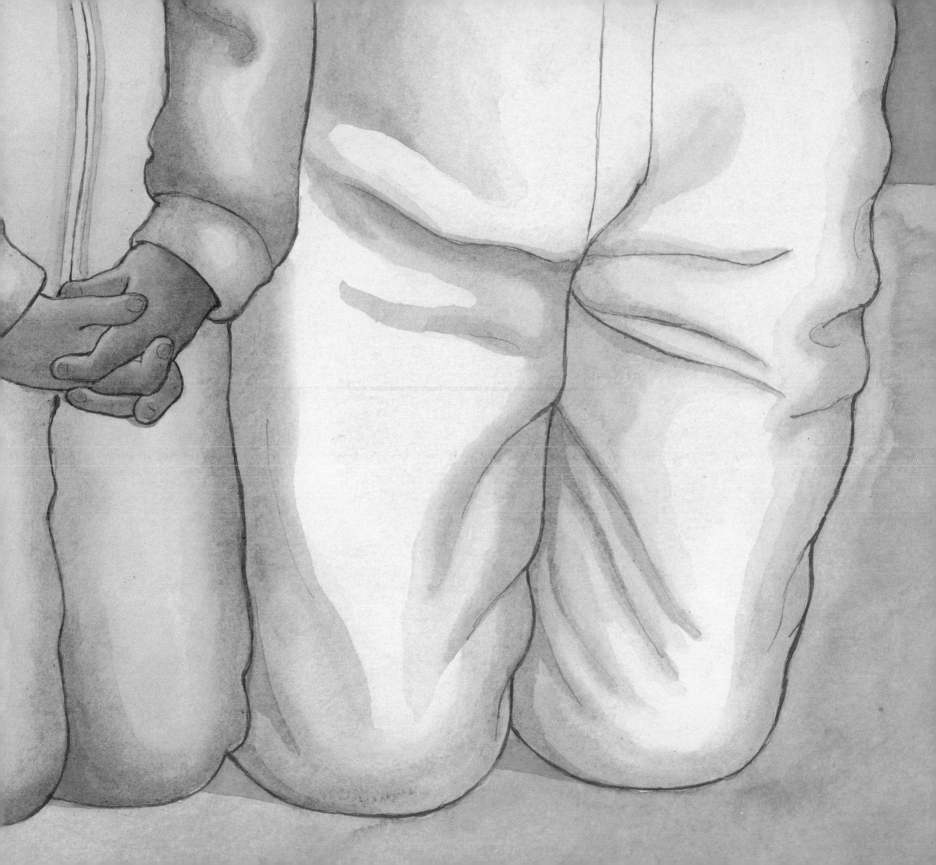

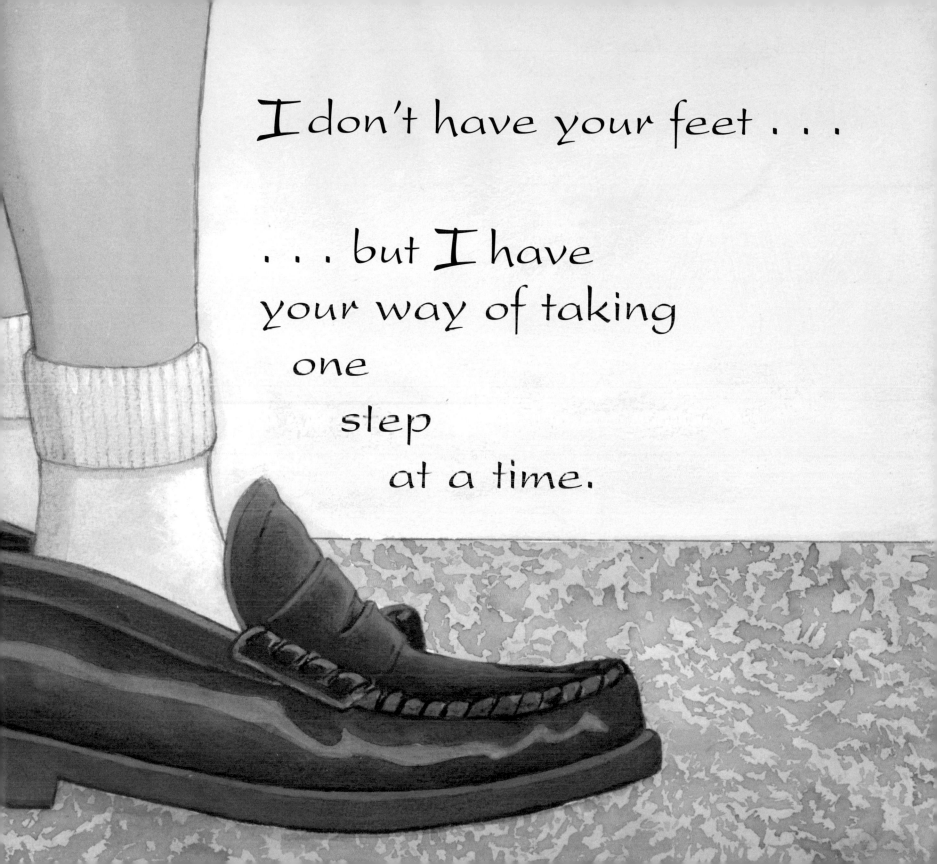

I don't have your feet . . .

. . . but I have
your way of taking
   one
      step
         at a time.

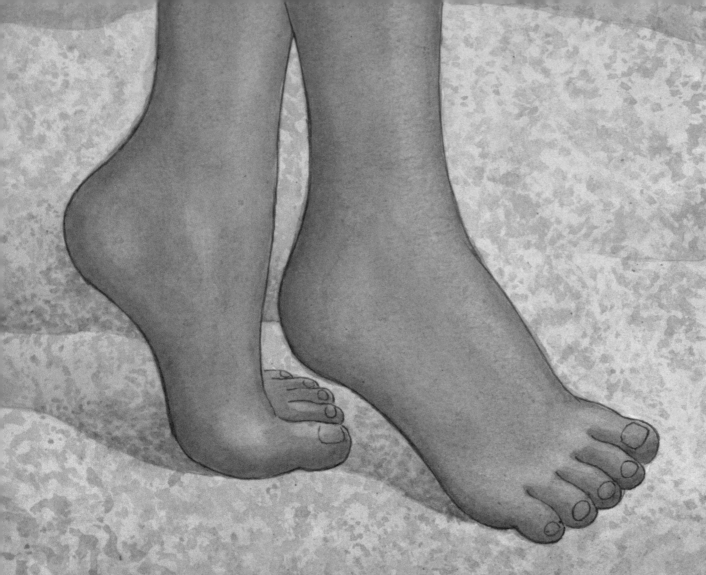

I don't have your toes . . .

. . . but I have your way of
dancing through life.

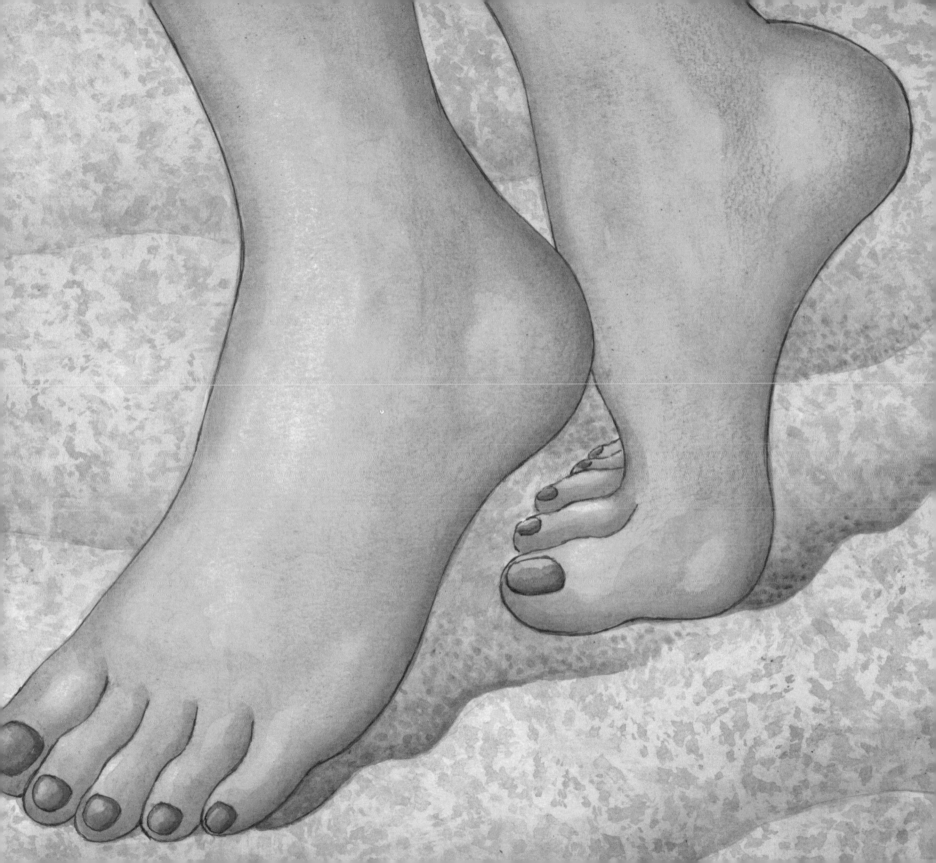

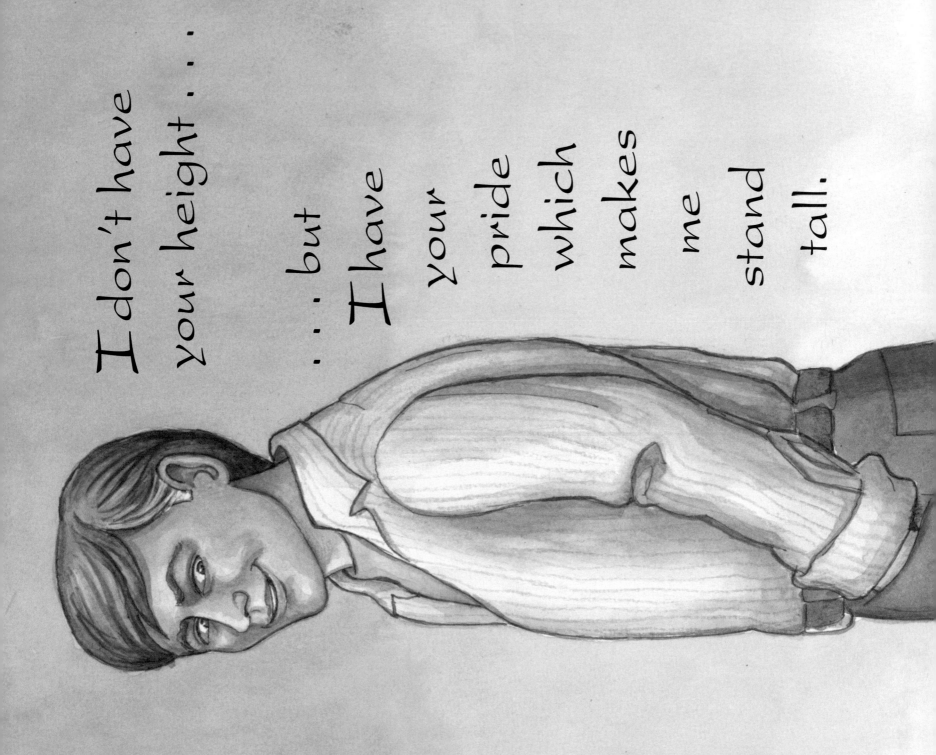

I don't have
your smile . . .

. . . but I have
your way of
making others
happy.

I don't have your voice . . .

. . . but I have
your way
of lifting spirits
with a song.

I don't have your face . . .

. . . but I know
you love the look
that is mine alone.

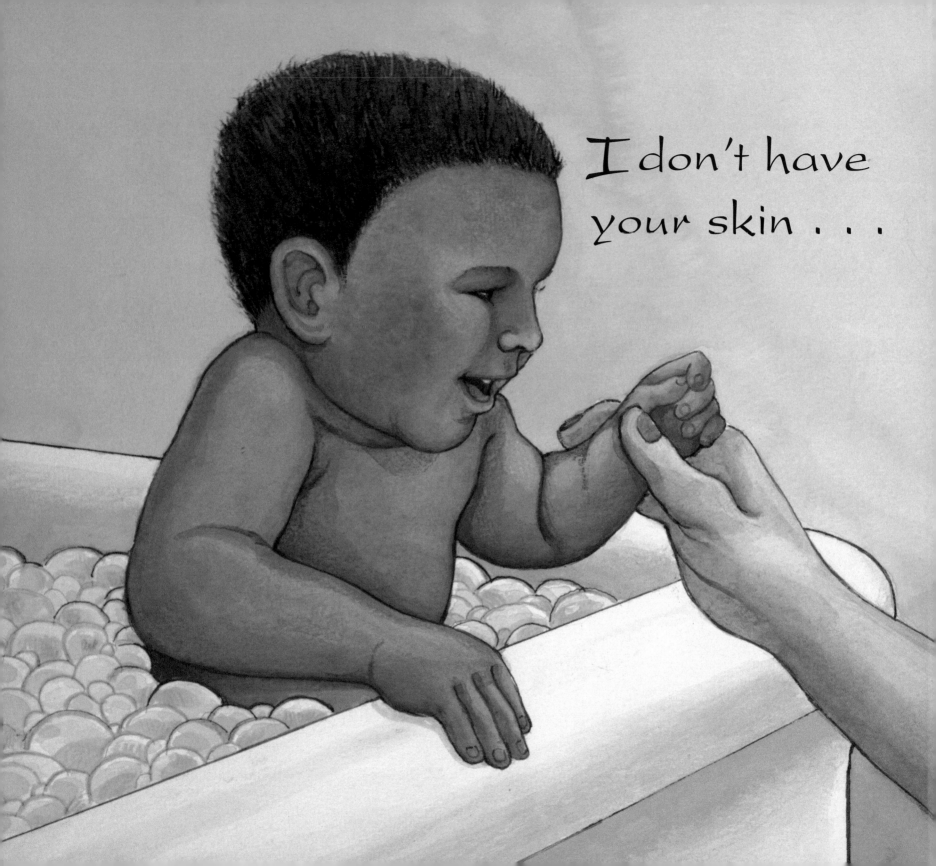

I don't have your skin . . .

. . . but
you have
taught me
what's inside
is most important.

I don't look like you
on the outside . . .

. . . but I look inside
and in our hearts
we are
the same.